Unforgivable

By: Davis Miller

It was like something like an orchestra that night. It was dark and windy during that fateful evening. The darkness was the conductor, the wind was the woodwind section and the banging doors were the brass section.

It was one o'clock in the morning. Scott Timble was tossing and turning in my bed, having a nightmare.

Violet Fyers, Shelby Ocle, and Jocelyn Farmicheal had already snuck from their mama's and papa's houses by this time. They were going to the old, abandoned building, a few miles from town. The rain started not long after Scott saw Violet at seven o'clock, and Scott

Timble tried to ring the Fyer's home, but no one picked up.

The three girls were all wet and dirty by the time they made it to the old deli out past town. From what bass been collected, Jocelyn brought the candles and the rug. Shelby obtained the lighter and the bowl. Finally, Violet came with the book. No one remembers what it was called, but everyone knew it was evil.

The banging doors brought solace to Violet and Shelby. To Jocelyn, it brought fear and apprehension. Jocelyn squeaked and shouted as the doors slammed shut.

"If you're too cowardly to do this, then leave Jocelyn. You don't belong with us, anyway." That came from Shelby.

"S-S-Shut up," Jocelyn yelled.

"Shut it you two!" Violet said with such aggression.

"Come over here and help me," Violet demanded.

They came over with trepidation. In the cold, damp, mossy, room, where every time they took a step, you could hear the wet moss in the stone.

Jocelyn unfolded the rug, and she put it on the driest sport she could. As Jocelyn was doing her job, Shelby placed the candles carefully onto the rug in the four corners. It was a dusty and black rug. Basic, but durable.

All three of them were in the circle at this point. Jocelyn was having a panic attack and the other two girls knew it.

"You're either with us or against us. Calm the fuck down or else." Violet snapped.

"I-I-I'm in."

Violet took a knife from her coat and gave it to Jocelyn.

"You first, Jocelyn. Prove to us that you are one of us. Bleed into the bowl."

"Is this necessary?" Jocelyn asked, wanting to get out of this.

"Cut or we'll cut you, bitch." Shelby said.

It was now starting to thunder. It was like God himself knew what they were trying to do.

"DO, IT NOW, BITCH!" Both of them screamed.

With tears coming down her face, Jocelyn cut right at the vein that popped out onto her wrist.

Crimson was oozing out of Jocelyn's wrist. Jocelyn, with panic in her eyes and pain in her wrist, hid her emotions.

"Baby." Shelby scoffed.

"Take this and clean yourself up." Violet talking while she handed Jocelyn some gauze and cloth.

Jocelyn, now holding her arm, and trying not to scream, did as she was told. She applied the gauze and covered it with a cloth. The circle was back together.

"Your turn, Shelby." Violet's words had a strange echo inside of the dump that was once a business.

Shelby took the knife, and not to be outdone with someone she deemed pathetic, went much deeper than Jocelyn and she could feel the pain of her wrist

With a cackle as loud as the thunder, Shelby once again thought about how she had outdone Jocelyn and how she was the second in command. With great glee, she applied the gauze and the cloth. To her, it symbolized another victory.

With both of Shelby's and Jocelyn's blood in the bowl, it was Violet's turn.

Like It was second nature to her, Violet cut her arm, and watched the blood flow into the bowl. With a grin on her face, she felt powerful.

The blood is now in the clear bowl that Shelby stole from her parent's kitchen. Thunder, as loud as a monkey with rabies, was still going.

Violet now pulled out her book and went to page seventy-two.

"Join hands."

They did as they were told as a kid would do for his parents.

"If either one of you two wants to chicken out, do it now."

"I'm not chicken," Shelby said.

At this point, you could feel bad about Jocelyn. She was sweaty as a fat man on the beach and was shaking like a man taking too many pills.

"I'm in." Jocelyn proclaimed.

"Are you sure?" Violet asked.

"Y-Y-Yes. I-I-I am s-s-sure." Jocelyn said this while getting a cold chill.

"Oh, just baby out. You're not going to do it." Shelby said.

"I'm not a baby!" Jocelyn couldn't help but yell.

"Sure you're not, just leave, you don't belong here." This, again, was Shelby.

"Shut up you two!" This wa s Violet talking.

"Are you with or against me?"

"With you." Shelby proclaim.

"Make a decision now, Jocelyn!" Violet demanded one, and she was going to get it.

Jocelyn grabbed their hands and replied with a yes.

Violet grabbed the book. "Repeat after me."

. "Oh, grand savior, please accept our offerings." Violet chanted

"Oh, grand savior, please accept our offerings." Shelby and Jocelyn reciprocated.

Jocelyn could feel her in heart this was wrong, but no one else was willing to allow her to be apart of their clique.

"Lucifer, save us. Use your might and power to destroy the non sinners!" They chanted once more.

With all of her strength, Violet shouted this. "Lucifer, my Lord, save us.!"

"Come forth" They shouted.

"Come forth our savior!" Violet chanted.

"Come forth our savior!" All three of them chanted.

Now, they all took a candle each and boiled the blood. Blood boiling like it was about to pop. They all three stared into the bowl of blood.

Nothing. All of that hard work, but no results.

"What do we do now?" Shelby asked

"I don't know." Jocelyn shivered and shook while saying this.

"Goddammit," Violet said.

Violet was now kicking the walls and the doors.

"WHY DIDN'T IT WORK?!?" Violet screamed.

"V-V-Violet, c-c-calm down." Shelby, clearly in fear of what Violet will do next.

"Yeah, Violet, stay calm before someone hears us."

"SHUT UP!" Violet screamed over and over again!

The rain and thunder outside were only getting worse.

"M-M-Maybe we should go home," Jocelyn said, but she would regret it soon after.

Violet, with a vengeance in her eyes and what could only be a demon possessing her, took the knife, grabbed Jocelyn by the throat, and put her head on the wall.

"I'll say when it's time to go home. Do you understand me?" Violet screamed.

Then, the dog started to bark.

"W-W-Who's out there?" This could only be one person. Harold Jenkins, the man who owns the property.

"Go get them, Rascal!" He shouted.

All three girls started to panic as it was still storming. What would they do? Lucky for them, ol' Rascal had a limp.

All three of them went through the back door, but it was stuck.

"Woof, woof, woof!" Rascal barked.

"I'm coming, Rascal!" The old man said.

The only thing that this dog was doing was infuriating Violet. It kept barking and barking outside the building until Violet had enough.

"I'm going to go shut that mutt up." She proclaimed.

She went outside in the rain, and she picked Rascal up by the scruff. She took out her knife, and without much of a fight, she started to stab Rascal repeatedly. Whimper after painful whimper. She looked back just to see the old man in her heels.

"What are you doing here? Who are you!?"

Violet turned to face the old bastard, clearly not in the right state of mind.

"Violet, we have to go!" Shelby yelled.

"Leave then! I'll be behind you!" Violet screeched.

Then, she took out her knife, and threw it towards the old man. Connecting with the old man's skull, he fell over in excruciating pain. Violet would come up to the old man, take the knife from his cranium, and slit his throat. The blood was pouring out from his throat.

"DIE ALREADY!" Violet screeched. JUST FUCKING DIE!"

GACK! The old man was choking!

Violet didn't have the decency to allow him to die in peace. She took her knife and started piercing through his stomach.

Eventually, the man died. Jocelyn screamed.

"Both of you, get him into the building. NOW!

They did what they were told, like animals in the circus. They were afraid of Violet now. She had just killed a man!

"Roll him into the carpet. We are burning this bitch down."

"Violet, you've gone insane! We need to call the cops!" Shelby said, after years of saying nothing to Violet about her behavior.

"SHUT UP AND HELP!"

They did as they were told in fear for their lives.

"A-A-Are we done, Violet?"

"No, each of you take a hammer and smash him. Make nothing recognizable!"

This caused Jocelyn to gasp. How could someone do this? She was struck with fear, but she needed to live.

"JUST DO IT!" Violet raged on with blood all across her face. Her eyes looked like the eyes of Satan. All over her body was Harold's blood.

They did as they were told, but neither one of them wanted any part of this. Every time Jocelyn would hit him with her hammer, she would cry a little.

"DON'T YOU START CRYING! GIVE ME THE HAMMER AND LEAVE, BABY!"

"I-I-I'm sorry!" Jocelyn whimpered as she ran from the old deli to her house.

"Violet, we need to go!" Shelby whimpered.

Violet stopped to admired her handy work. His guts were spilled to his side. You could see bits of his skull and brain matter now. The giant laceration on his neck was as deep as a grave. His knee caps and bones on his arms were all busted. Intestines on the floor. Eyeballs were crushed and chewed to honor Satan.

"I hope you take this as a fitting sacrifice, my Lord Satan."

Violet took out her lighter and started a fire onto the old building. Shelby and Violet went home not saying a word until they separated.

Shelby was startled, while Violet was proud. Shelby knew this side of Violet was going to come out one day, but she didn't believe it was going to be this day.

The monster inside of Violet is quite a hateful one. Violet's hatred for the world stemmed from abuse and being pushed around. She was a loner by heart. People that were like Shelby and Jocelyn would have to helped her, but no. It gave her a power that she shouldn't have had.

The power over a person who is easily brainwashed is a very dangerous ability. Manipulation is key. Shelby had no real friends until she met Violet. Now, she is under the control of Violet Fyers.

Jocelyn had no choice, but to join up with Violet and Shelby. She was, in her mind, unlikable. She was bullied in multiple schools, and at one point, was homeschooled.

Now that the monster has been unleashed inside of Violet, can anyone stop it? No one knows the answer even to this day. All everyone knew that all hell was going to break loose.

All three of them made it home unharmed physically, but the psychological toll was intense. People themselves were afraid of Violet.

A lot of people in town never believed in demons or angels until that day. Now, it's as real as God.

"Did I please you Satan?" Violet whispered to herself, trying to sleep.

The fire was still burning when they made it home. From the ashes rose a monster that would haunt this town forever.

Once they all separated, Jocelyn went to the nearest pay phone, put in three quarters, and called the authorities. This is the transcript of the call.

"Hello, yes, I would like to report a murder and fire." Jocelyn said with vertigo.

"Yes, okay, stay calm." The operator said. Who am I speaking to?"

This caused Jocelyn to pause. "I'd rather keep my identity a secret."

"Okay where is the fire located and who was murdered?"

"It's at the old deli and I think it's Harold Jenkins who died! I have to go! I can't be caught. Bye." Jocelyn hung up the phone and started running.

Detective Scott Timble arrives at the scene to a roaring fire. The fire was burning and scorching hot. Smoke arose into the sky that night.

Once the fire was stopped, Scott and other policeman got to work.

On the next day, Jocelyn was the first to awake that morning. Now, bearing a gash on her left arm, she awoke from her slumber in a pool of her own sweat, thinking what happened last night was just a nightmare. She had black marks under her eyes and her eyes were bloodshot.

"Was last night a dream?" She said to herself.

She was so close to falling over, so she went to d some coffee. Black, just like last night. What really did happen last night?

She looked out the window of her home. She started to shake.

"Should I even go to school today?" She thought she whispered that, but she talked in her normal voice.

"I might as well." She said.

She couldn't stop thinking about Violet, the dog, and the old man. "How could she have done that?

She clenched her teeth and thought to herself. "What if she kills me next?"

Jocelyn, panicking at the thought of seeing Violet, began panic once again. What she saw next would haunt her.

"Woof, woof, woof!" Was that the dog from last night? Jocelyn turned away in fear. "YOU'RE DEAD! GO AWAY!"

"Woof!"

After several minutes of barking, Jocelyn finally turned around. She knew what she was going to see, and she was kind of right.

The dog, whose name had to be named Rascal was beaten and bleeding. The dog was missing an eye and its jaw was broken off. Patches of hair were missing, and he also had a wimp. "Woof!"

"I-I-IM s-sorry, doggie!" Jocelyn was a squeamish girl. Her hair was red and she had a lot of freckles. She was pale and the only one to feel any remorse for any of this. She also had blue eyes.

She could feel tears in her aquamarine eyes, so she went upstairs. She applied her makeup and got dressed up for school.

She sighed silently and left her house. She knew that she would have to see Violet and Shelby. She also knew that Violet would kill her if she ever mentioned last night to anyone.

She stepped on the wet grass, and she started walking, knowing that she will have to confront those two soon. Very soon.

She gulped as hard as she could. Her mouth was dry, because of the anxiety she was feeling. Oh, what she would make last night only a dream.

She made it to the bus stop, but what she saw horrified her. Both Violet and Shelby were on the bus, just glaring at her as if nothing had happened. She begrudgingly got onto the bus and took a seat.

Shelby awoke. Dazed from last night's events, just like Jocelyn, she hid knew of her covers. She couldn't believe what had happened with Violet last night. "What was that?"

Eventually, she came out of the covers and got dressed. Her boney body was like that of someone on methamphetamine. She looked in the mirror, reflecting upon herself. She didn't know what to think. She had read and black hair, along with a sharp nose, and hazelnut eyes.

She was quite sweaty, so she showered. While in the shower, the water turned to blood. This caused her to panic and scream. Nobody heard her, because she became hoarse after last night. Then, what she saw next, petrified her.

The old man's severed head was in her hands. It started to turn, and before she knew it, it was floating in the air. It was, in a way, like a jellyfish. Where his neck should've been, veins were floating underneath his head.

She looked in her hand and saw an eyeball looking into her soul. She looked into the eyeball and saw Violet. "What?" She said slowly.

Eventually, the head intensively, kept staring at her. She got out of the shower, got dressed, and ran into the living room, knowing no one was home.

What she saw next sent her into a frenzy. It was… Violet… with a knife intensively. "Violet, it's me, S-Shelby."

The figure that appeared as Violet moved swiftly and elegantly as one would associate with a ballroom dancer. It grabbed her by the throat and forcefully banged Shelby's head into the wall. "You listen to me. You tell no one what happened with the old man and dog. If you do, I will find out, and I will kill you myself. Understood?"

"Y-Y-Yes. What about J-J-Jocelyn?" Shelby asked.

"Oh, I have plans for her," Violet said in a way that caused Shelby to be concerned for Jocelyn.

"Who's side are you on?" Violet finally asked.

"Y-Yours." Shelby muttered.

That's when the figure disappeared. Shelby was dazed and confused. She packed her stuff for school and ran to the bus stop. She was panting, but she made it with ten minutes to spare. Ten minutes with her thoughts.

She looked around, but nothing was there. She had no makeup on, and she was wearing a tank top and black jeans. She was sweating quite profusely when the bus arrived.

She got onto bus, hoping that she could find a seat away from Violet. Unfortunately, no luck. Violet called her over to where she was sitting.

Shelby went over and took her normal seat with Violet, but there was something different. Something darker. What could it be? Whatever it was, it was frightening and not to be messed with.

"Follow my instructions to the letter." Violet ordered.

That's when Violet told Shelby the plan.

As the wheels on the bus went into gear, the horrific details were revealed.

Violet was the last one to wake from a blissful slumber. She felt like she was on top of the world. She could still taste the blood from the old man. She pulled out the still bloody knife from her pocket and licked it for joy. She went and found a bowl to show that she was in control and what happened at that building will be kept a secret.

After the spells were done, Violet got into the shower. While feeling the smooth touch of the hot water, it made her giggle. It reminded her of the old man's blood and how it flowed out of him like a river.

She got out of the shower and admired her body.

the body every girl her age wanted. Big boobs, fat ass, look good without makeup. "I am your perfect vessel. Oh, mighty Lucifer, lend me your power."

She felt powerful knowing that Satan walked with her. Now, it was time to keep her lackeys at bay. She conjured the spells once she got home, and they were to go off once she gave the signal. After that, she left for school, joy in her heart, and Satan by her side.

Along the way, she noticed a change in herself. She felt more powerful like she was a ventriloquist with her puppet. Her puppets, of course, were Jocelyn and Shelby. Oh, poor Jocelyn. She made that foolish decision to join the group. She decided to go out with them last night. She needed a plan to keep them both quiet. That's when it came to her.

She ran back to her house and prepared the plan. She used a dream spell to fuck with Shelby and to keep her in check. Also, she knew that Shelby would be too scared to go to the anyone about it.

She just barely made to the bus, but she didn't mind. School was just school to her. She went to classes when she felt like it. She believed that she was one of Satan's chosen ones.

I saw her that day, walking like she always did. I thought about saying hi to her, but even I felt something dark. What scared me was my wife. She was holding a cross in her hands and praying one of her payers.

"Oh, Jesus Christ, my Lord and savior, please protect me from the darkness I sense in my world. Please protect my family, my friends, my husband, and myself. Thank you, Lord. Amen." The former Mrs. Timble said.

I saw this, and immediately went into my house. I consoled my wife and took her to our bed. I lie her down with her cross. I went back to you, outside. By then, Violet was long gone.

"Why do those old people staring at me? Whatever. It's not important." Violet said to herself.

Scott Timble got ready for work that day, thinking about that girl, Violet. She used to be so sweet. I can't think about that right now.

As Scott was going to work, I saw Violet get on her bus. She smiled at me, and at that moment, I was terrified. I knew I should have done something, but I don't know what.

Once Violet got onto the bus, she grabbed something. I could see it on the edge of my right eye. I should have done something, but what?

Violet knew that if her plan doesn't work, she may be doomed. Her confidence, though was high.

Now, all three of them are on the bus. It was an unusually silent day. You can feel the tension between Shelby and Jocelyn. Shelby was crunched in the inside by Violet and Jocelyn was sitting alone across from them. Just like normal.

Shelby could feel her heart beating like it was going to explode out of her chest. She knew the plan, but it didn't feel right about it. Truthfully, she didn't want to go along with it, but she was still fazed from earlier. She gulped and was shaking from the sheer anxiety of what Violet had told her to do.

Jocelyn, meanwhile, was one second from crying her eyes out. All she wanted to do was look out the window, but that wasn't happening. Violet tapped on her shoulder, and stared her right in the eyes, and said this.

"Us three are to meet in the girl's bathroom during lunch. Got it you two?"

"Yes." They both whispered.

Then, complete silence. Shelby and Jocelyn went back to looking out the windows. Violet, meanwhile went back to feeling the knife in her bag.

Mile after mile, wheels turning, seconds ticking. It started to rain profusely. Jocelyn looked out the window as if she was pondering running away from them. Could she, though? Was she that brave? Jocelyn grabbed her necklace, thinking about her mother, and what she would do next. Mowing her mother would want her to be strong from heaven.

The silence of the bus was getting to Violet. It felt like everyone knew what happened last night, and they were going to report her to the authorities. Violet quite liked the sound of the rain. It reminded her of blood. Like, the way it dripped down windows reminded her of the old man's blood dripping from his throat. Violet closed her eyes, so she could replay that moment over and over again. It made her tingle.

Jocelyn and Shelby stared at Violet. They were both thinking the same thing. What is wrong with her? They looked at her in fear. As if they were mice and Violet was a cat on their tails. Jocelyn sniffled and Shelby shook at the very same second.

"Do I sense a problem, you two?" Violet asked.

"N-N-No." They both said, and went back to starting outside the windows.

They were making the turn into their high school when Violet made herself clear.

"If either one of you doesn't show up, then you both shall be punished."

"Get off the bus!" The bus driver shouted.

As people were getting off the bus, Violet made sure that they were the last ones off. They were now at Breekson High School. Violet had the confidence of a bird who had just caught its first worm.

Meanwhile, Jocelyn and Shelby were terrified of what was going to happen on this day. They would have to wait until eleven thirty until they found out.

Jocelyn wanted so badly to run, but Violet had a grip on her shirt. That told her all she needed to know. She was stuck in this situation. She began a silent prayer in her hair.

All three of them entered the school. With fear, with trepidation, and with power.

First and second period that day were mind numbingly slow. Tick, tock, tick, tock. All three of them were watching the clock. Racing thoughts through their minds, sweat flowing down their necks.

All Jocelyn could see was white. She was panic-stricken about the way Violet looked at her. Looking into Violet's eyes made her uneasy, but what was it about them? It was like staring Death in the eyes and coming back to tell the tale. All Jocelyn could do was look at the clock. What was it about this day that scared her?

It was still raining that day. Thunder and lightning, even the trees were about to tumble. Jocelyn stared out there, like a deer in headlights. She knew something was up, but what could she do to find out. Nothing. She couldn't do anything. She was at the mercy of her own mind.

Shelby was lost. Would she did the decent thing or will she obey Violet just like usual? While everyone in her class was talking, she was in deep thought. Twirling her hair and clinching her fists, she was quite anxious. Her teeth were chattering. "What am I going to do?" She said to herself.

Violet was alone in the girl's bathroom, smoking a cigarette and fidgeting with her knife. She took several drags, enjoying the escape from reality the nicotine offered her. She took out her knife and cut a vertical line on her tongue with it. She loved the taste of blood, and she was going to get her fill on this day.

Jocelyn looked at the clock. Ten minutes. Jocelyn, then had a full fledged panic attack. It felt like her heart was going to burst through her chest. She felt like throwing up her guts, but she knew she had to be strong. She grabbed the ruby necklace from her mother and said a silent prayer. She grabbed her stomach. Then, the bell rang. That must have been the longest ten minutes of her life. She was now off to the girl's bathroom.

Jocelyn just stared at the clock once the bell rang. She knew what was coming. She knew she had to tell Jocelyn, but why? Ever since Jocelyn joined the group, she felt like she didn't belong. Shelby knew that Jocelyn was a

Christian, but the fact that Jocelyn would betray her religion for them, should mean something.

At that moment, she came back from her daze. What she saw, made her panic. It was Jocelyn walking, slowly, to the girl's bathroom. "Does she know?" She asked herself. All she wanted to do at that moment was yell for Jocelyn and get her to safety. For some reason, her voice was gone. She tried to tell for Jocelyn, but she couldn't.

She eventually was set free from her invisible trap. She gasped for air. She was about to cry when she realized that she was all alone in the hallway. Nobody would hear her. Nobody would console her. It was just her. She went towards the girl's bathroom.

"J-J-Jocelyn!" She said in a hoarse voice. Jocelyn didn't hear or see her. Jocelyn went in the bathroom, and Shelby followed with fear. They were all three in the bathroom together.

"V-Violet?" Shelby said, unknowing if what was about to happen.

"Is Shelby out there with you?" Violet asked with a calm, but frightening voice.

"N-Not yet. Oh, wait, I hear someone. It's Shelby."

"Good. Shelby, lock the door." Violet demanded.

Shelby did as she was told. She knew not to disobey Violet or else she'd be getting punished swiftly enough.

Finally, Violet came out of her sanctuary in the bathroom stall. You could smell the fresh cigarette on her clothes. With that same anger in her eyes from last night, Violet pulled out the knife that she's had hidden since this morning.

"Now, Jocelyn, you must be taught a lesson." Violet said.

"W-What?"

"We are doing this to keep you in line."

"M-Maybe, we don't have to do this, Violet." Shelby whispered almost to herself.

"Do I need to teach you a lesson too, Shelby?" Violet asked without mercy.

"No, I'll shut up." Shelby said with fear in her heart."

"Good, now grab Jocelyn." Violet told her.

Though she didn't have any desire to see Jocelyn hurt, she grabbed Jocelyn by the hair, and put her on her knees. Jocelyn could here a faint whisper. "I-I'm sorry, Jocelyn. Please forgive me."

Violet could hear this somehow, so she drove the knife into Jocelyn's thigh and went down to her knee. There was meat banging out of the gash, and this seemed to give Violet even more desire to keep going.

Shelby wanted to cry and run from this, but she knew Violet would get to her somehow, someway. Shelby did think about releasing Jocelyn, but she knew what would have happened.

The laceration was bleeding even worse now, but Violet wasn't done. She took the knife and she split open Jocelyn's other thigh.

"Someone please help!" Jocelyn screamed.

"Get me the toilet paper, Shelby." Shelby did as she was told, but she knew this wasn't right. Even if her and Jocelyn didn't like each other very much, she knew that she could do nothing. Blood was everywhere, Jocelyn's meat was all over her thighs, and she had the toilet paper in her mouth acting like a gag.

Jocelyn started to cry, and she started to fight to get free. She almost escaped the remorseful clutch of Shelby, but Violet kicked her in the stomach, and all Jocelyn could do was lie there in pain.

Knock, knock, knock. Someone was at the restroom door. Jocelyn was begging for this person to see this insanity, so they could lock up Violet and Shelby for this. What she didn't understand was why was Shelby's grip so loose. Was she trying to let her go free. Was she willing to terminate any sort of trust Violet had with her, just so she could escape. Impossible, she thought.

Always a quick thinker, Violet threw herself and Jocelyn into the bathroom stall that she had just recently occupied, while whispering to Shelby to keep that person from sniffing around too much.

Shelby was able to clean up some of the blood before she heard it again. Knock, knock, knock. This caused Shelby to panic and open the door. This is when things would get worse for Jocelyn.

Jocelyn tried to escape Violet's clutch, but all that managed to do was enrage Violet even more. Violet took the knife and stabbed into Jocelyn's stomach. All Jocelyn could do at this point was bleed and scream, but no one heard. Eventually, whoever that girl was that had to use the bathroom so bad, left without noticing a thing.

Shelby was about to run out when Violet saw her. Shelby looked into Violet's eyes and knew that if she left and told someone, she was dead meat. Shelby stayed, but she was not spared.

"I know what you were trying to do, and quite frankly, I don't appreciate you fucking with my lesson on obedience. You must pay as well Shelby. Take your shirt off or else." Violet said with such grit and determination.

She just stared at Violet like Violet was a dinosaur. She was in shock and awe of what Violet just asked her. She could see into Violets eyes. She did as she was told after a couple of minutes. "Please, let this end soon, God, please."

She said that to herself. It was like Violet's senses were stronger, because she miraculously heard that.

"Bend over." Violet demanded with the cold voice of the devil. "DO IT OR ELSE!"

Shelby complied, and now it was her turn. What was Violet going to do to her? Shelby was facing a weak, bloody, barely conscious Jocelyn. Jocelyn's eyes were barely open. All she saw was Shelby lying down on her knees and hands. Next, she saw that Violet had her knife, and she started to stab at the spine of Shelby's. Shelby was in quite a lot of pain. All Jocelyn could do was crawl towards her and offer her hand. Now, Shelby and Jocelyn were holding hands, like they were on the same side of this.

Violet saw the hand holding and went into rage. She stabbed harder and harder into Shelby's spine until her arms grew weary from all that work. She took a step back to appreciate her work. She had one more strike in her, so she went for the two hands that were together. Neither one of them were conscious at the point.

Brrrring! Brrrring! Brrrrying! Lunch was over. Violet took a look at herself in the mirror, thinking about how she was going to get out of this. She lit a cigarette and started to think. "What do I do?"

Eventually, a light bulb went off. She needed to get these two out of the school without being caught. She started to clean. She took toilet paper and paper towels and cleaned off all of the blood, something that took her several minutes. She put the clothes back on Shelby and Jocelyn. She actually decided to use the window to the roof of the school. One by one she took the bodies up the outside ladder to the roof of the school. She was worn out at this point. She didn't know how much she had left until she saw the dumpster. She formulated a plan at this point. What she did was toss the bodies into the dumpster and then herself. The garbage truck would then take all three of them to the junkyard, which was only a mile or two from her home.

Everything that Violet needed to happen happened. The dump truck arrived on time, took them to the junkyard, and from there on she took both bodies to her house. Yes, she would have to hide them for the time being. She made sure her family wasn't home, and went to the basement. There was so much clutter and junk, to the point where this wasn't recognizable. Yes, she could hide them here until they awoke. That was what she did. One at a time, Shelby first and then Jocelyn, she took the bodies to her home and into the basement. She put Shelby into a grandfather clock. Due to Shelby's short build, she went in easily. Now, Jocelyn. Violet had to look for a few minutes to find somewhere to put Jocelyn. Eventually, she found a spot for her. An old couch that should have been thrown out years ago. Yes, it was infested with bed bugs, but to Violet, this was just Jocelyn. Violet moved the couch cushions and ripped apart the bedding inside of the couch. She picked up Jocelyn, with every muscle she had, and put her into the couch. She placed the bedding and couch cushions into place. Oh, yes, this was, she thought.

She would go on upstairs and wash off the blood off of herself. The hot water felt good against her skin. She took the knife that did the stabbing into the shower with her. It was like, she was obsessed with this item now. She took the knife into both of her hands and cut her bottom lip open. As the blood was flowing down her chin, mixed with the black for her lipstick, she knew what this meant. She knew, eventually, she will be caught. In her own sick, twisted, mind, she wanted to be caught. She wanted the recognition of a Dahmer or Bundy. She smiled at that. Oh, what stories this town would tell.

She would check every hour, she thought. Check to see if either of them have awoken, died, or moved an inch. When they did, there was going to be order and discipline. This was a dictatorship, not a partnership. What she said goes, and she was quite sure that those two have learned that lesson.

She started thinking. What would happen if her mother or father came home, at this point? She didn't really care. She lit another cigarette and decided to take a nap. Oh, what a joyous day she thought. What could make this day any better? She really couldn't decide. She went to bed knowing what happened in the bathroom would be safe. She knew that neither two of them had the courage to fess up to anyone, because of their fear of what she would do. This caused Violet to grin. Even Violet herself was shocked about that smile. Violet got so excited to the point where she couldn't get to sleep. Oh, what she had on this day, and it may not be done yet. Violet fulfilled her promise to keep checking on them every hour, but they've not awoken yet. After two o'clock in the morning, she went to sleep, but the sleep didn't last wrong. Eventually, one of the girls stirred, and Violet knew it. She was on her way down to the basement. Of course, she had the knife.

Jocelyn awoke in a pool of her own sweat, unknowing of her location or how she even got here. She heard a noise, so she stayed quiet. Someone was in there with her. She heard a noise that sound like someone was trapped inside of wood. Jocelyn got up slowly and surveyed the area. Just junk and clutter, but she knew where the noise was coming from. It was coming from a worn out grandfather clock. It was like someone was trying to break free. Jocelyn decided to help this person. Once she got up, she was in complete, agonizing, pain. She knew not to scream, but her legs were wobbly. She got on her knees and crawled towards the clock.

Eventually, she made it to the clock. She opened it to a sight that surprised her. Her doing that caused her hand to hurt. It was

Shelby. Why was she there? The last thing Jocelyn could remember was Violet stabbing her in the stomach. What happened to Shelby? Did Shelby take a beating for her?

Shelby fell out of the grandfather clock and onto Jocelyn. Shelby was barely able to move her torso at this point, and it was quite obvious that she was in pain. Shelby was as still as a board. Is she dead? Jocelyn thought. No, she's just sleeping. Jocelyn tried so hard to make herself believe that. The door to the basement opened, and Jocelyn knew exactly who it was.

It was Violet with the same look from before as well. "Have you learned your lesson, Jocelyn? Or do I need to do what I did to you all over again?"

At this point, Shelby got cold and stiff. She was near death. She started to murmur a little, but not much.

"V-Violet, p-please. She n-needs help. She's going to d-die! DO YOU HAVE NO HEART!?" Jocelyn pleaded.

"SHUT UP BEFORE I STAB YOU AGAIN!" Violet screamed at the top of her lungs.

"Have you learned your lesson, Jocelyn? If not, I can easily hurt you again." Violet asked.

Jocelyn looked into the eyes of Violet. Wow, she thought. This is what we've unleashed. How can we stop her? She thought to herself.

"You can't. Now answer up, or I'm leaving you two down here." Violet demanded.

"We-We-We have learned out lesson." After saying this, Jocelyn put her head down in defeat. Starting to cry now, she felt like she let Shelby down. Shelby was barely moving. "We need to get her to a hospital! Please, Violet!"

"No! We'll treat her here. Come upstairs."

Jocelyn stood up, put Shelby's arm around her shoulders, and made it upstairs. Jocelyn was at the point where she was going to fall if she didn't get the weight of Shelby off of her.

"Sit her in that chair." Violet demanded.

Jocelyn did as she was told. Violet began to stitch Shelby's spine and torso up, which took an hour. Next she went to the laceration in her hand and that was it. Shelby was all stitches up.

"Your turn." Violet told Jocelyn. Jocelyn sat down and let Violet get to work. Violet made a discovery that would shock the minds of serial killers. There were bed bugs growing inside of Jocelyn's body.

"I'm going to have to get something for bugs. Don't move."

"Okay. I won't." Jocelyn said in pain.

At this point, Jocelyn could feel something biting into her stomach. She wanted to know what it was, so she took a look. Violet was right. Bugs, and there was an army of them.

Violet was back with the bug spray. "Don't scream." As she said that, she sprayed the solution into Jocelyn's body. Jocelyn couldn't help, but to let out a little cry. Violet put her hands onto Jocelyn's mouth. Violet kept spraying until she all of the openings covered. Violet began stitching Jocelyn's wounds.

Shelby was barely breathing at this point. Her body was a stitched up mess. Finally, for the first time in what felt like years, Jocelyn could breath calmly. They were all sweaty, tired, and worn out.

"You need to go home." Violet finally said after what felt like years of silence.

"How are we supposed to get there? I mean, look at Shelby, she's hurt bad." Jocelyn asked.

"Shelby stays here. Her parents don't care what she does or not. Your parents don't like me, so you need to get home, and think of an alibi. Don't say a thing about what happened or else."

"Okay." Jocelyn said.

"Go, now!" Violet demanded.

This caused Jocelyn to hurry out of there. What was she thinking, she thought. "Why did I leave Shelby back there?"

She couldn't think of one reason why. Was it because she was scared? Or was it, because of how Shelby had always treated her until today? She didn't know, but what she did know was that she needed to hurry home. It was four in the morning, and she didn't know how she was going to explain this to her father. As she was walking she kept formulating scenarios in her mind about what she would say. None of them were good at all.

It was still quite dark, but Jocelyn felt like someone was watching her. She didn't know who, but she would have put her money on Violet. She kept walking down the path towards her home when she heard dogs barking.

"Woof! Woof! Woof!" They all were shouting. This caused me to wake up and find out who that was. I loaded my shotgun and went outside.

"Hello?" Scott Timble said. There was no response, but I could hear the shoes dragging onto the gravel.

"Either you reveal yourself or I'll shoot. It's up to you."

This caused Jocelyn to panic and reveal herself to me.

"I-I'm s-sorry, Mr. Timble. It's just me. Jocelyn Farmicheal! Please don't shoot!"

"Jocelyn, what are you doing out this late!?" Scott aked.

"I-I don't know!" Jocelyn said in a panic frenzy.

"Calm down, Jocelyn. I'll take you home. Let me get my coat."

He went inside, got his coat, kissed his wife on the cheek, and got his keys. Jocelyn and Scott went into my truck and started on towards her house. I could see that she was panicking.

"Calm down, Jocelyn. It's alright. I'll talk to your parents. Might even say that you were helping me out, if you act good." Mr. Timble said.

"You would do that for me. I'm just a girl." She said.

"Oh, stop! You're not just a girl! You're Jocelyn freaking Farmicheal! Don't put yourself down like that. For Christ's sake! I'm sorry. I shouldn't have raised my voice, but you need to stop putting yourself down! You may not be the skinniest or the smartest, but you're a nice girl."

"T-T-Thank you, Mr. Timble. I won't do it again." She said in a low, soft, voice.

"Stop calling me Mr. Timble. That was my father, his father, and so on. Please, call me Scott." He said in a voice that didn't show his true emotion. He felt bad for this girl. Clearly, something was wrong, but he couldn't put his finger on it. That's when he saw her hand.

"What happened there, Jocelyn?" He asked in a cold, monotone, voice. "Please don't lie to me.

This caused whatever calmness and tranquility that Jocelyn just had to fade. How could she have been so stupid!? She looked at her hand, and tried again and again to make an excuse. Eventually, this is what she said.

"Oh, this, I has am accident in cooking class, with a knife." She said. "You know how girls my age are. Sometimes accidents happen."

He knew she was lying. He knew something was wrong, but he knew he couldn't call her out on it. "Well, next time, be more careful, sweetheart. You don't want that to be permanent." He said.

To Jocelyn, this meant victory. She actually convinced a cop that this was just an accident. Hmm… maybe this could be a start of something, but when she started to think a little, she panicked. Her thoughts raced just like race horses. Did I just like to a cop!? Should she tell the truth. That's when it all dawned on her. The attack. The pain she felt that day when no one was there to save her. She was alone. There's no point of telling the police, because they wouldn't be able to stop Violet. They'd only enrage her even more. That thought sent a chill down Jocelyn's spine. What was she doing I'm a car with a cop!? What if Violet finds out about this!? What if she already knew. This caused Jocelyn to have a panic attack. Thud, thud, thud, was all she heard. The beating of her heart against her chest was amplified. Thud, thud, thud, over and over again. At this point, Jocelyn was seriously thinking about running away from all of this, but she knew she would be found. By Violet, who would probably kill her, by her parents who would beat her, by the police who would interrogate her, a rapist, a murderer, she didn't fucking know! Jocelyn couldn't breathe now. Wheeze after wheeze, she was gasping for air.

"Hey, are you okay, Jocelyn. Jocelyn, speak to me!" He said, talking without a clue of what's going on. Oh, Lord, should I pull over. We only have a few turns, so I sped up a little, and we made it to Jocelyn's house. I ran to the door, and I knocked as swiftly as I could. On the wooden porch, I was greeted with an obese man who's probably had too much to drink tonight.

"May I help you, sir?" He said in a tone that even made me jumpy. This man really thought he could give me this kind of attitude, and get away with it. Well, he did, for now.

"Your daughter, come quick!" Scott said. I ran while he was "speed walking," according to him to my truck. This is when he saw Jocelyn. He knew what this was, so he told me.

"Just a panic attack. No big deal. All she needs is her pill and some sleep. Thinking about it, where had she been? You better not lie to me, boy, if you know what's good for your health and safety."

"Mr. Farmichael, she was helping me a dog d my farm. I'm sorry it's so late, but I thought she needed some time away from you, that's all. Now, lose your tone voice, or I'll make you lose it. Take your daughter inside, give her the medicine, and stop drinking for the night. You really should value your daughter more than a bottle!"

After I said this, Mr. Farmichael took Jocelyn by the wrist, and pulled her into their house. "Stay away from my daughter, piggy! If you know what's good for yak!" He said. He slammed the door shut. Better get out of here, I thought. Without looking back, I went to my truck, started the ignition, and started for home, feeling like a lard of cow dung. I could tell that man was not fit to care for a child.

"Please forgive me, Jocelyn" I whispered inside my truck, just before I got home. Now, I need a drink myself.

That night, I believe Jocelyn saw God. I had a bad feeling just by the smell of her father's breath. Jocelyn could barely walk when I saw her.

Once, Dalton Farmichael got his daughter into his house, he pulled off his belt. Jocelyn, still wheezing and panicking got beat. Dalton made Jocelyn pull her pants down, and he whipped her. Each lashing Jocelyn got, she would cry louder and louder. This would cause that crazy son of a bitch just grew angrier and angrier. Growing rage that was only strengthened due to his daughter being a disrespectful and rude bitch. Dalton Farmichael still blames Jocelyn for her mother's death. The pregnancy of Jocelyn caused Fiona Farmicheal to die. Dalton wanted Jocelyn aborted, but Fiona refused. Fiona would throw up blood, lost her hair daily due to the stress of pregnancy, and would bleed from her mouth, nose, and privates during that time.

It was like God, himself, did not want Jocelyn born. Why, though? She's a nice girl. It wasn't her fault that her mother was dead. That night, I could not sleep. I tossed and turned like a casket during an earthquake. What was I missing? I didn't know. I still don't. All I knew was that I had to work that next morning.

Violet had Shelby in her grasp. Would she kill her? No, not yet. This was a time to make up and get back on track. Shelby woke up in a pool of sweat and urine the next day. Violet hid her in room, because her family never went in there. That considered her style as unholy and that she was a sinner.

Once Shelby woke up, she thought she was in hell. She saw Violet immediately, which caused a great sense of panic. Not to the levels of

Jocelyn's, but still quite bad. Shelby remembered what happened, and wanted no part of Violet.

"You're awake I see." Violet said.

Shelby couldn't move at all, so she knew she was at the mercy of Violet. "Y-Yeah. Where am I? Shelby asked.

"You're at my house. Jocelyn ran away, so I had to heal you. What I did was wrong, but so is what Jocelyn did. The moment Jocelyn awoke, she ran. I was there for you. I was still here to stitch you together and to heal you, even after you betrayed me." Violet said softly that even caught Shelby off guard.

Shelby went unconscious again. With just her and her thoughts, Shelby contemplated what she heard from Violet. Did Jocelyn really leave her? Was Violet the one who healed and mended her. She knew Jocelyn was no good, but was she that despicable? Shelby started to have nightmares.

The three of them were in the bathroom again, but this time it was different. Shelby was still getting stabbed, but it was Jocelyn holding the knife! Stab, stab, stab! Bits of flesh and bone flying out of Shelby's back. Violet was in the corner, crying from the assault that Shelby had caused her. Violet moved her hands, and what Shelby saw made her jerk awake. Violet had no eyes!

"W-W-What was that?" Shelby whispered. Was that the truth or a lie Violet had made up? She didn't know, but what she did know was that she was hurting and she can't move very well. She tried to sit up, but her frail body couldn't hold her spine in that position.

"That's why you're like this. I conjured up a spell to show you what you may have forgotten. You're safe now. She can't hurt you." Violet said. Violet had this all planned out.

"That can't be true" Shelby thought. This was Shelby in a deep state of thinking. She didn't know what it who to believe. All she knew was that she was in so much pain.

"I can heal you, but it would come at a price." Violet had said. Yes, all of this was coming together.

"W-W-What do you want?" Shelby whispered . Truly, she couldn't take the pain anymore. Her spine was disfigured to the point where, if she didn't listen to Violet, then it would never be healed.

"You must partake in a blood oath with me. You must swear on your life to me and to always be by my side eternally. You must agree to never betray me. Do we have a deal?" Violet asked.

"O-O-Okay." Shelby said after several minutes of silence." She was petrified of what would happen if she said no. "I-I'm in."

"Good." Violet said. Violet took out her knife and began the blood oath. They cut their arms, and that was that.

The deal in place, Violet knew she Shelby wrapped in her fingers. She knew she would need her later on. She made sure to get the deal done.

Shelby, still not sure of what really happened in that day in school, was quite tense.

She didn't trust Violet all the way, but she did trust her more than most people. "We had a deal." Shelby mentioned. Violet would heal her that night.

The police report came back. It said what Scott had feared. Harold Jenkins was dead, and the fire was arson, not natural. What to do? He thought.

.”Who called that fateful night?” He murmured, drinking a shot of bourbon in his office. The next morning he made some phone calls. He had found out that the caller was a younger female, probably in high school.

Scott called the high school and asked if there was anyone who would or could do such a thing. He was given one name. Violet Fyers.

He did his research and find out that Violet was a problem child. Violet had done victimless and crimes, but she was still a person of interest.

Scott would interview her at the police station, and Violet let it slip. She had two friends .She put Shelby and Jocelyn in the middle of this. Scott would interview all of them separately, and realize that it was Jocelyn was the one who called for help on that night, but why would she report a fire and murder that she was a suspect in? He didn’t know, still doesn't, but it would be a while longer for him to close this case. In the mean time, he started to plan.

Shelby, Violet, and Jocelyn were not seen in school for the next two weeks. Eventually, Shelby went home, but had very strict directions from Violet. Violet had fabricated a story to Shelby's parents about a gang of raccoons. They believed her instantly, and they took Shelby home from there. They debated taking her to the emergency room to see if the raccoons had rabies or anything, but decided to take Shelby home instead.

Shelby heard a tirade of stuff from her father that night. The father wanted answers, and he was going to find out one way or the other. He locked her in her room, and didn't let her our for two weeks. Violet kept communication going between herself and Shelby through their minds. They'd communicate spiritually by the connection they had through the blood oath.

Violet knew what she was doing. She was plotting every scenario just like you would in a game of chess. The one wildcard was Jocelyn. How was Violet to keep little Jocelyn wrapped in her fingers? Violet went through every scenario, and finally had her answer. It was risky, but Violet knew her secrets must stay secrets.

Jocelyn was at the mercy of her father for those two weeks. Her father would beat her over and over with his belt. Jocelyn would cry and scream for hours, but there was no one who wanted, or could, save her. She was left with nothing. Nobody. Her whole body was covered in bruises and cuts. Jocelyn wasn't allowed to eat, so she was quite frail. That night, though, the monster inside of her awoke.

That night, her father came to her room while she was sleeping and tired her up. This awoke Jocelyn, and she tried to break free, but couldn't. Jocelyn was deeply frightened what sick deed her father had planned for her.

Dalton Farmichael would end up torturing his daughter that night. Cut after agonizing cut. Lacerations all over her body. Dalton had her tied up and at his mercy. This, she recalled was just like what happened with Violet. How could they do this, she thought. She screamed and begged him to stop, but he didn't. Excuse my French, but that son of a bitch was getting a sick pleasure that only a crazy nut case could get. This would last for hours, and after he was done., he untied Jocelyn and left the door unlocked. He saw this as a triumph, and he went to get the good bourbon and chugged the bottle. He went out to get more bourbon, and he was back within an hour.

Jocelyn prayed that night, harder than ever before. She was in tears, and had no idea of what she was supposed to do. She prayed for a warrior to come and save her from all of this. In the deep silence, she could hear the clock tick, the air flow among the trees, and the rain drizzling on that cold, fateful, night. Everything became silent. Jocelyn tried to pull herself up to stand, but failed. At this point, she wanted death.

The, supposed, man known as Farmichael would get even more drunk once he got home. He made himself something to eat, ate it, and fell asleep on the recliner with the old television on. He must have been dreaming lovely dreams, because he was so giddy and happy I was told. The man was a drunk, but no one thought he would go as far as doing what he did.

How could a man do that to a poor little girl, let alone his daughter? You'd have to be a crazed son of a, excuse my French. I'll try not to slur like that throughout the rest of this story. I'm a modest man, but even I could smell the evil on that man.

Sc9tt took a drink out of my cup of sweet tea. Wow, I thought. "It's been that long. I still don't understand everything about what happened. How could you do the things that these people have done. The sad thing is that the story is not over. I digress.

The clock struck twelve for Dalton Farmichael. The entity known as vengeance went into the kitchen and got a butcher's knife. It limped throughout the house with the knife. Oh, Mr. Farmichael was in for a surprise on that night. Hood over it's bead, it just wanted redemption.

Dalton Farmichael was asleep dreaming merry dreams that night. He was giggling and laughing like he was in paradise. The box television was on, the beige wallpaper was crisp. The air was making the door bang and slam against its hinges. It was like the night at the beginning of this story, wasn't it?

Vengeance was coming. She paraded around the house, butcher's knife in hand, was still going through the house. The entity went upstairs to Jocelyn's room, and just stared. It had a vision of what happened that night. The lashings, the beatings, and the rape. The entity knew why it was called here. I was here to kill the man who had done this.

Mr. Farmichael woke up to this entity in front of him. Thinking it's just a hallucination caused by the liquor. He went back to sleep, with his beer belly and scruffy beard, covered in sweat. He was dreaming at this point.

Some where in the woods, the son of a bitch was in terror. He didn't know where he was or how he got there. All he knew was that he was alone. He started to move, but it felt like both of his feet were broken. He looked down to see what was going on, and he saw was bug after bug, chewing and gnawing at his two legs. In a frantic state, he started brushing the bugs off of his legs, but to no avail. He tried to use his strength to run, but it failed. He started screaming, but that made the bugs angrier. They kept biting and going up his body until he was fully covered in them critters.

In the real world, he was throwing up puke and snot. Eventually he started chocking on his vomit, but he awoke in time to save himself. He went to the toilet puked there up something he did not expect. Bugs. He threw up bug after bug into his toilet. He was screaming for Jocelyn to come and save him, but that was not to be.

Eventually, it all stopped. With blood coming out of his throat, he spit in the sink. Thinking it was all a dream, he looked in mirror, and saw something that nearly gave him a heart attack. He saw the entity for what it truly is. He tried to scream, but nothing would come out. He tried throwing stuff at it to try to stop it from coming closer.

His voice came back. "P-P-Please show mercy!" He begged and begged, but that was not meant to be. Now, the bugs were coming back up the toilet. Dalton tried to run, but he couldn't get far. He made it to his truck, but he couldn't start it. His legs looked like a mountain lion had been feasting upon them.

He looked to his right, and he saw this entity. He got out of the truck just in time, but he didn't make it much further. Back inside his house, to be exact. He didn't know what to do. All he knew was that he needed protection. He went to his room and got his switch blade. He thought he was ready for what that son of a bitch had planned.

Standing face to face with the hooded figure, Dalton Farmichael went all for broke. He ran up to it and tried to use his switchblade, but it did no damage. The blade just burnt and evaporated into air. This sent a chill down Dalton's throat. He knew that he was near death, but that didn't stop him. He took out his shotgun and started firing shots, but still, no damage.

The figure just smiled. Oh, he saw it this time. This infuriated him to the point where he used his gun as a bat. No damage was done. Dalton started to scream and have a guest fit.

"WHY WON'T YOU DIE, BITCH!?" Dalton yelled while firing shot after shot. Eventually, Dalton Farmichael could not keep going at that pace. He eventually ran out of his room, and into the bathroom, but he blocked it this time. "It won't get me now. I'll just wait it out until morning." He said to himself.

He finally had a minute to catch his breath, but it for only a millisecond, because the door to the bathroom flew open. With fear and vertigo in him, he just stood there. "W-W-What are you?" He asked, thinking he was entitled to an answer. The figure didn't talk. It just led the bug to the bathroom, and they began to feast once more. He didn't know what to do, so he crawled away. Begging for this figure to stop and go away, he started to cry. He didn't see that coming, but his life was on the line.

"W-W-Why are you doing this?" He begged. The figure did not answer. The bugs not eating and chewing his body. Blood was oozing all over him. Eventually, the entity told them to stop. Thinking he had just beaten death, he tried to run past the figure, but this failed as well. The figure took the switchblade and butcher's knife, and began ripping body parts out of Mr. Farmichael. The pancreas, liver, brain, feet, and muscles were all taken from the scene. What would this entity want with all that. I didn't know. There was one more thing as well.

The hooded figure took off it's hood to reveal itself to Mr. Farmichael. He must have been in a great state of shock, because, once we found his eyes, and saw what his final expression was... a state of shock and fear. It was like he had seen God and Lucifer himself, and didn't live to tell the tale.

At the crime scene, Scott Timble scoured and some more to find evidence as to who did, or could, do this. There was nothing. No murder weapon and barely a body. The strangest part was that no one heard anything. Not one person could even tell me when the hooded figure arrived, let alone who it was. This felt like a cold case waiting to happen. At that moment, Scott then had a thought. Jocelyn.

Jocelyn awoke that morning feeling as good as new. Her body didn't hurt anymore. She went downstairs to find her father, but she was in for the surprise of her life. Her father wouldn't budge from his recliner. Usually, when she said something, he'd turn or move. Jocelyn went closer and tried again, but it failed. She went in front of her father, and saw why he wasn't responding. There he was with his own switchblade in his throat. Jocelyn was shocked. She didn't cry, though. She threw up, because this was only the second time she had seen a body this mutilated.

Once, Scott was called into the area, my first priority was Jocelyn, but he couldn't find her. She was no where to be found, and that freaked all of the police out. Was this a hostage situation? Nobody knew. All we knew was that a girl was missing, and we didn't have time to fool around. They got to work.

Jocelyn decided to run before anyone arrived. She picked up her essentials and left what used to be her home. She didn't know where to go. She decided to go on to the next town over and order a train ticket as far from here as possible. She didn't want to look back. First the crap with Violet, and now this...

Scott felt for her. She must have been traumatized by all of this. I didn't know what I could do to help her, and it made me feel horrible. I just wanted to give her the biggest hug possible and have her over for dinner. That wasn't how the story ended, unfortunately. Let's keep going.

Jocelyn ran from her former home that morning in a frenzy. Knowing that she would be the first to be blamed and interrogated, she ran with a fury unrivaled like a lion. She kept running until she was wheezing like that night when Mr. Timble took her home. She didn't care anymore. She knew that she couldn't live in Breekson any longer. Whether it was Violet or the fact she would be the first suspect in her father's murder, she knew it was time to run.

Scott looked all over town for her, but she wasn't anywhere, so I went to the home of the Flyers'. I knocked on their door, expecting to be answered by one of Violet's parents, but I was incorrect. The person who answered the door was Violet Fyers.

Once she answered, he asked her if she knew where Jocelyn was. She said no, and that was that. Violet shut the door in my face. That conversation gave me chills down my spine, and it still does. Scott could tell at that very moment that Violet Fyers was going to be a problem with our investigation. Did she have something to do with the murder of Farmicheal or the fire at the abandoned deli? I couldn't rule anything out, especially after Jocelyn was acting weird the night Scott drove her home.

After hearing that Jocelyn had ran away, this caused a tirade from Violet. She smashed glass around the house. How could she be gone? Violet, knowing that Jocelyn telling the cop about what happened that night in the abandoned building could put her in jail, she went to her room, and packed up essentials that she would need to find Jocelyn. She would leave at midnight, and she would go to the next town over.

Midnight came, and Violet left on the dot. She started down the path to the road, but there was one problem. She forgot about the detective's house being on the way to the road, or she would have taken a different path. She growled to herself, but stayed on the current route. Thinking the detective and his wife must be asleep, she ran through their yard. This would cause the animals to start barking, so I came out with my gun. I didn't see anything pit of the ordinary, so I went back inside and slept. Dreaming of dreams so horrific that I sweated profusely.

Shelby awoke knowing something was wrong. She looked at the window to see if someone was out there, and there was. It was

Violet. Shelby knew what was going on, because she was also questioned by Detective Timble. What was Violet doing out so late, though? She opened her window, and came outside once Violet wanted her to.

"Let's go." Violet had said in a voice that even scared Shelby. Sure, Jocelyn and herself had problems, but that was no excuse to kill. Violet convinced Shelby to go by brute force. Shelby wanted to scream for help, but she couldn't. She was, once again, at the mercy of Violet. Violet had dragged her by the hand, the hand in which had a scar from the attack.

Jocelyn, having no where to go, slept in the woods, under a tree. She knew that Violet was you to come for her, and she was ready. She was ready to die, at this point. She had seen two dead bodies, been stabbed to the point where she couldn't walk, been beaten, and raped. Why on earth would I want to live? She thought to herself. The fire she had built was cackling and the bugs were chirping. If this was her last night alive, she was going to enjoy it. Jocelyn put her hood on to stay warm, in which it succeeded in doing so. She went to sleep softly that night, knowing what was going to happen. Knowing that Violet was on her trail.

Scott awoke that next morning knowing where he had to go and when I had to be there. He awoke before his wife did, so he got going. Scott started his truck, and he went to the next town over, trying to beat the clock. He sped and went through red lights like I was a maniac running from police. He knew time was not on my side, so he kept going until he made it.

Shelby and Violet made it into the forest where Jocelyn was sleeping soundly. They walked quietly and swiftly through the forest. Violet knew they were close, she could feel it. They tried not to make noise, but that wasn't possible. Shelby, with maybe an hour's sleep that night, was to the point to exhaustion. Violet walked such grace, like a lion looking for its prey. Violet had her pocket knife out. She knew that she was going to kill Jocelyn that day. She was quite confident in that fact.

Jocelyn could sense their presences. She got up, and kept moving. Eventually she made it out of the forest and into the next town. She headed for the train station. Once there, she ordered a ticket to Leonie, England. Over two thousand miles from Breekson. She knew that she had to settle business. She went back into the forest and waited. She was ready to end this with Violet. It's now or never.

Violet and Shelby finally made it to the spot where Jocelyn had slept last night. No one was there, so Violet told Shelby to run, and they ran. They ran a straight path and made it into town. Shelby and Violet went back into the forest and went looking for Jocelyn. Violet knew she was still in the forest. Jocelyn just needed to be found.

Jocelyn was hidden among the trees, waiting for Violet to come into sight. Jocelyn was holding the train ticket on one hand and her knife in the other. This was it, she thought. Her heart was racing, but she couldn't think about that right now. All she could think about was killing Violet and being done with her old life. She was done getting hurt.

Scott made it to the next town around ten in the morning. Being unfamiliar with this area, he asked around for Jocelyn, but no one had seen her. Eventually, I was starting to give up, until I thought of something. She probably wasn't showing her face. How could he have been so stupid!? Also, if she went one town over, was she planning to go farther away. He ran to the train station, and asked if they had seen a little girl or someone in a hood. They said yes and pointed me to the forest. They also said they saw two other girls leave and go back in the forest. Scott had to act quickly. Hr ran into the forest, unsure of what I was going to find. He ran and ran yelling Jocelyn's name, but it wasn't Jocelyn I found. It was Violet!

"What are you ladies doing here?" he asked quizzically.

Acting like he was unworthy of an answer, Violet scoffed and said that it was none of my business and that he should leave while they let me.

This infuriated him. "You two are under arrest for the murder of Dalton Farmichael and Harold Jenkins."

"You aren't going to arrest us. In fact, you're not going to make it out of this forest." Violet said. She took out her pocket knife and told Shelby to tackle me down, but Shelby wouldn't do it. This caused Violet to flare up with emotions. She threw her knife right into his shoulder, so be screeched in pain when it first hit my shoulder. He pulled out the knife, and he grabbed the wound. Violet walked towards him, and picked up the knife. What was she planning? He tried to reach for my gun, but Violet had he by the throat. She had Scott by the throat, but he overpowered her, and threw her ro the ground. I thought I had hr defeated, but it was at that point when Shelby stabbed me in the back with the knife.

Violet got up and retrieved the knife from Shelby. "Are you ready to die, bitch?" Violet asked with a touch of anger. Her face was red and the dark circles under her eyes only showed the rage behind those eyes. Even he was afraid for my life at this point. I didn't know what was about to happen, and I could honestly say that I was struck by fear.

Violet took out her knife like she was about to cut him up. He tried to step back, but Shelby was in my way. She blocked me, so he couldn't go anywhere. Violet took the knife and put a laceration through my stomach. Scott started to cough up blood, and I tried to break free. Shelby had me in a tight grip, and he was so weak to the point where he could not move. He tried to scream for help, but only the trees could hear my pleas. Violet kept stabbing and stabbing to the point where my blood was all over her body and my stomach was nothing more than artwork in Violet's twisted mind.

All Violet wanted to do in among the trees was to kill this man. She kept stabbing and stabbing until she couldn't stab any longer. The grass was covered in blood, as was Violet's body. Shelby tended to Violet while I was barely breathing and fighting for my life. Then, a miracle happened.

As Violet was about to deliver the kill shot, until she heard a twig break. While bleeding all over, Scott saw what Dalton Farmichael must have seen during his final moments. A hooded figure came from the forest and threw a knife that nearly stabbed Violet in her back. Who was this?

Nearing the point of collapsing, all I see was my life flashing through my eyes. All the way from my birth to that very day. My first day on the force and my graduation of the police academy. Finally, I had accepted death, and my savior was standing before me.

The hooded figure just stood there staring into Violet's cold, unforgiving, eyes. You could cut the tension with a knife. Second after precious second passed. It was like one of those old western movies where both sides wait for the other person to make the first move. Once the sun radiated through the trees, they ran for it all.

Violet took her knife out and started to run towards the figure. The figure, standing, rushed at towards Violet, and when they met, Violet tried to stab the figure. Violet missed, and the figure threw her down to the ground and started kicking her stomach. The figure took Violet's knife and attempted to stab her, but the knife landed into the dirt, not touching Violet at all. During the failed stab attempt, Violet was able to get up and bite the figure's leg. There was no scream of pain or a plea for help. The figure took Violet by the hair and bear her head against the tree. Violet was bleeding, but she escaped the figure's grasp. Violet ran to the knife, and she was able to get control of it. Once she did, she went into a fighting position with the knife in her hand.

The hooded figure ran towards Violet, unknowing that Violet reclaimed her knife. The figure ran to Violet, but Violet was ready. The figure swung at Violet, but Violet took the knife and stabbed the figure in the stomach. Violet got on top of the figure and attempted to stab it. That didn't succeed. The figure moved out of the just in time, but Violet was able to rip the hood to reveal… Jocelyn!

They stared at one another. This is the first time all three of them were together after the day of the incident at school. Both Shelby and Violet stared at Jocelyn. They never though she would kill someone. They could barely breathe, Violet and Jocelyn.

Jocelyn, grabbing her stomach, pleaded with Shelby. "Shelby, why are you taking her side? I was the one who protected you that day!"

Infuriated by Jocelyn's words, Shelby and Violet ran to Jocelyn and began beating her. Kick after kick, punch after punch, Jocelyn was in so much pain, but she didn't quit fighting. She pushed than away and began swinging at Violet. Shelby, still loyal to Violet, and dove at Jocelyn's legs. The beating resumed, but Jocelyn would not be deterred.

Eventually, Jocelyn was able to get up and put up a fight. Punch after punch between Violet, Shelby, and Jocelyn, this was a worthy battle to die in. They kept going past their breaking points. This was when Violet and Shelby drew back.

"S-Shelby, w-w-why? I protected you." Jocelyn had said in a voice that was near death. Blood was running down Jocelyn's stomach and onto her legs, she knew this was her last chance..

Violet went up to Jocelyn and kicked her right into her wound, aggravating the wound. "Liar!" Violet had shouted. "All you are is a liar!" Violet had yelled. This mad Shelby uncomfortable, so Violet turned around, and said, "We have a deal! Don't cross me, again!"

This caused Shelby to remember everything. She remembered everything for how it truly happened. She remembered what Violet had done to her and Jocelyn. This caused Shelby to panic. She knew what the right thing was, but she didn't want to believe it. She shook her head left to right over and over again until she got dizzy.

Jocelyn, near death, revealed the truth to Shelby. She showed her the scar on her hand. It was the same scar that Shelby had. Shelby panicked and nearly collapsed. She did what she thought was right. She ran to aid Jocelyn. She didn't make it.

This caused a volcano to erupt inside of Violet. Violet grabbed Shelby by the hair and throat, slit her throat, and threw her to the ground. Jocelyn ran go Shelby as fast as she could while holding her stomach. Shelby, near death, said her last words. "I'm sorry." Shelby was now dead. This sent a fire inside of Jocelyn.

Jocelyn got up, shaking from the blood loss, got up, and ran towards Violet. Violet, with her killer instinct now back, grabbed Jocelyn by the hair, and was about to slit her throat, but she knew Jocelyn was weak, so she decided to play around with her. Violet released Jocelyn and threw her knife down. "Fight me." Violet said: Get up and fight."

Jocelyn got to the knife and stood up. She swung, a weak swing, so slow that Violet got a punch onto the stomach. Violet kneeled before Violet, so Violet took, the knife and attempted to slit Jocelyn's throat.

Jocelyn fell down in time to prevent Violet from doing anymore damage. Jocelyn crawled away from Violet, but failed. Violet took fist smashed Jocelyn's face into the dirt. Jocelyn's nose was bleeding, possibly broken. Violet started to run her skull intro the dirt.

Violet had her knife, stalking her prey. She went for the final blow, but Jocelyn dodged just in time. Jocelyn grabbed Violet's throat and begun strangling her. Jocelyn's hands suffocating Violet, Violet was fighting for her life. Violet eventually broke free of Jocelyn's grip and threw her into the ground once again.

Violet started scratching Jocelyn's face, but Jocelyn was able to get free by finding a rock, grasping it, and hitting Violet in the eye. Violet fell backward and grabbed her eye in pain. She screamed at the top of her lungs. "You bitch! That fucking hurt!"

Now, they were both in front of each other. Violet ran for Jocelyn, but Jocelyn caught Violet with her father's switchblade. Right into the stomach. Jocelyn then got down on her knees and forced the blade into Violet's throat. Violet bled a lot of blood, so Jocelyn kept stabbing at Violet's body. Shelby was now covered in blood, but she was the last one left. She was the last woman standing. This caused Jocelyn to think. I guess in Jocelyn's eyes, she was the true monster.

Jocelyn got up and tended to her wounds. She went to my side and grabbed my phone. From what I've gathered, she called an ambulance. She did not stay the whole time, though. Scott, among others, believe Jocelyn really got on that train and didn't look back.

The End:

www.ingramcontent.com/pod-product-compliance
Lightning Source LLC
Chambersburg PA
CBHW061709130726

47996CB00006B/2231